BLOOD PROPHECY

MARCUS
ORIGINS

BARB JONES

This is a work of fiction. Names, characters, places, and incidents are products of the author's imagination or are used fictitiously and are not to be construed as real. Any resemblance to actual events, locations, organizations, or person, living or dead, is entirely coincidental.

World Castle Publishing, LLC

Pensacola, Florida
Copyright © Barb Jones 2015
Print ISBN: 9781629892580
eBook ISBN: 9781629892597
First Edition World Castle Publishing, LLC June 1, 2015
http://www.worldcastlepublishing.com

Licensing Notes

Cover: Steven J. Catizone
Editor: Maxine Bringenberg

Acknowledgments

Welcome to the world of Blood Prophecy. Meet Marcus, one of the sexiest vampires in this series. I wanted to give my fans a more personal look into the lives of the main characters. Their lives were so intertwined in the prophecy long before they met.

This novella is really dedicated to each and every fan of the Blood Prophecy series, as well as to the Queen's Champions. I have a truly amazing team that makes all of this possible for me. If you enjoy this story of Marcus, you will love the series and upcoming books. I write these for each of you.

A special dedication to my two favorite fans: Arianna and Kaiden, my children.

CHAPTER ONE

Spain, 1793

Marcus had been living on the streets for some time, ever since the banker had cast him out because he could not afford the promissory note that the old clockmaker left him with. The old man had died of the palsy but had lived a very full life, and Marcus had loved him as any son would.

Marcus was cold and hungry, and his once nice garments were nothing but shreds now. He was a strong young man with olive colored skin, thick, dark hair, and a sharp, pointed nose that was perfectly centered in the middle of his face. His dark eyes matched his hair perfectly, and though he was considered to be a vagrant now, his eyes still showed hope and promise. His tender heart loved all of mankind, and there was never a day in which hatred filled him. Even when the banker arrived and threw him and his belongings out of the clockmaker's shop, he still loved life. He had also been the most eligible and good looking bachelor in Spain until he became what he was today.

Marcus remained in the alley and heard a carriage come his way and suddenly stop. A door opened and a young woman emerged. Her long reddish hair was full of curls, her pale white skin showed absolute perfection, and her thin red lips were inviting to be kissed. She took her time but he did not move, watching as she approached him and realizing that he recognized her. She had come into the clock shop every so often.

Eliza was a single woman, though new to town in the last two years. Marcus knew some of her story, but not all of it. She was from Catalon and had almost died in childbirth. Miraculously, Eliza pulled through the ordeal, but people assumed, including Marcus, that the baby had not survived because a child was never with Eliza.

Eliza's eyes met his and she smiled. Marcus's palms began to sweat just a little, but he managed to smile back. "Miss Eliza. Welcome. H…h…how may I help you today?"

She had a wonderful laugh as she said, "I need a clock for my parlor. But it can't be loud. I would like it delivered to the estate. It's time I fixed it up, don't you think? But you aren't in your shop."

Her green eyes stared right into his soul. As he looked back at her, he found himself glancing at her perfect face. Not a blemish in sight or a hair out of place. Her red hair was never in a womanly up do, but more of a young girl's style. Her body was enticing, slender at the waist with a bosom that was bursting at the seams. She showed no signs of modesty as did the other women in the town. Marcus felt that she knew she was very beautiful, and was confident in her appearance. That confidence spoke to his man parts loudly, causing him to stay where he was.

Eliza cleared her throat, waiting for a response from him. Marcus had a hard time speaking to her but finally managed to. "I have not yet seen your estate, but I'm sure we can find you the perfect clock. Unfortunately, I am no longer employed. And it's been quite some time since I've washed and eaten. You would be better off asking someone else."

Her fingers touched Marcus's fingertips before he could turn around, and tingles shook his body. He felt something pulling him towards her. Closer. He looked right into her eyes and her soft voice spoke to his mind. *Follow me, sweet boy. Leave this life and join me today.*

He left the alleyway and never looked back.

***

Eliza held Marcus's hand as they roamed through the alleyways until she was able to find a dark corner. She threw him against the wall and kissed his lips. His body responded in kind and she ripped open his shirt. She could feel his heart beating and his breathing was getting heavier. Eliza knew that he was attracted to her, and she took this moment to smell his scent. His carotid artery was calling her name.

Her right hand moved his chin so that the artery was exposed. Arching her neck, her fangs became elongated and she ripped into his skin, drinking enough of his blood to turn him.

When she was finished, she bit into her wrist and fed him her blood. With her clean hand, she gripped the parchment that was in her pocket and read the words again.

A young man, dark haired and innocent, will become a blood drinker by the fair skinned woman. His heart will love her but she will only be his maker. His truest love will be born from the one who can be a soothsayer and more. Her love for him will bind his fate. He is the shepherd of the child who is to be an instrument. But this man will lust for blood like no other. His rage and lust must become part of him, but not all of him.

This was all that she had and her master's instructions were clear. Find the boy and turn him. But she also knew she had to train him. She watched him begin the painful change. It brought back memories of her change, but something was different. Could it be part of this prophecy that she held in her hand? Kabos made sure that she understood the prophecy and what was to come.

Marcus's body crumpled to the street and lay there motionless. Suddenly, his body arched and contorted in different ways. Bones were cracking, and the mark of the vampire burned into his flesh. Another mark, a strange one, was inherently burned into him as well, and soon disappeared. But Eliza was able to catch a good look at it and noticed that it was the mark of the witches. She then knew he was the one.

Marcus lay on the ground. The blood that had been spilled was going back into his body and his flesh was healing. Eliza looked at him with lust and knew that she needed to take him home. He was her charge now, and it was up to her to train him, teach him, and let him find his way. She even felt that they could remain in Flanders, feeding when needed, and no one would be the wiser.

***

Marcus woke to a darkened room in a massive, heavy bed with the sheets to his waist. He could tell that he was not clothed, but he was hungry. He longed for something, but did not know what. On the bedside table sat a beautiful off-white card with flowing black calligraphy. On the card were the words Ring Me. Next to the card was an ornate silver bell. Reaching for it, Marcus rang the bell.

A servant opened the door within moments and brought him a gold cup. The cup was ancient looking with a thin ruby line around the top, and the stem was the matching ruby color. It was beautiful yet sturdy. "Sir, the lady said that you must drink this in order to live." Handing the cup to him, the servant bowed and left the room. Marcus looked at the cup and then peered inside. The smell told him it was not wine nor water, but something more potent. It had a clean, fresh smell, but was not something he'd ever drank before. But as his nostrils smelled the red liquid, his lips began to tremble. His gums began to have a sharp pinching pain as his teeth extended and became pointed. Marcus's tongue flickered at the cup, barely touching the liquid, but after it did, he held the cup in two hands and gulped the contents in seconds. Blood trickled from the cup down his chin, and he used the back of his hand to wipe his mouth. His thirst was now satisfied, and he threw the cup against the wall. Inside him a rage began to stir, but it was not strong. He felt like his insides were twisting and his body was aching for something, but he knew not what it wanted.

The door opened and it was the woman, Eliza. She came to him and sat on the bed. Marcus looked at her and was in love. He assumed it was love because she was so beautiful. He didn't think about taking her or kissing her, but wanted to do anything to make her happy. Eliza was his woman and that's all that he could fathom. Her hands stroked his hair and her fingers moved to his fangs. Marcus was a beautiful newborn, just waiting for pleasure. Her pleasure and instruction.

Eliza tore back the sheet that kept him from being exposed. Her hands ran against his body, touching him. Marcus felt every finger, every touch. He longed to kiss her lips, unafraid of her. Lips touched, hands moved, and bodies intertwined. Marcus felt the heat of their bodies rise, and near his thigh, her teeth sank into his flesh. It was a small pinch but once he felt her teeth in his leg, his body relaxed. He could even feel the coldness of her fangs against his skin. She drank of his blood and when she was finished, she showed him how to drink from her. Soon after, both became intoxicated on blood.

When they were done, both laid back in the bed, drunk on bloodletting and sex.

Chapter Two

Eliza was dressed in evening attire. Her dress flowed out from her bodice, accentuating her hips and bosom. Marcus came down the stairs dressed with flair in a tuxedo. Both vampires were now bonded and ready to feed. As a newly turned vampire, Marcus was not able to control his emotions, and the minute he saw Eliza, he flew to her and ripped open her dress. Her breasts were exposed, nipples erect, and his fangs tore into her flesh as his eyes turned red. He was hungry and his appetite for her body became insatiable. Eliza responded in kind by feeding on him, but she exhibited self-control by not tearing at his clothing.

Lesson one was taught. Marcus had learned the art of bloodletting from his maker. But as young as he was, he did not have restraint. Eliza learned that he was impulsive and uncontrollable. But he was hers to master and she was glad for it.

Eliza spoke. "You will stop and stop NOW." Her voice emphasized the word NOW and was commanding. Her child had no choice but to obey.

***

Marcus hung his head and felt shame at the command. He didn't understand what he was and wasn't supposed to feel. But in a short time, he realized what he now was. He was a creature of the night, a cold blooded drinker, the one the drunk men told stories of to scare each other. He only drank blood now and his hunger was larger than before.

His hands gripped her neck and squeezed. Lifting her skirts, he found her center and drove right in. His length reached her point of ecstasy, and all Eliza could do was scream out in pleasure. He thrust into her faster and harder until her juices flowed down her leg. Servants did not enter the room because they knew all about newborn vampires and their need for sex, their need for blood and lust. Eliza screamed at him.

Marcus's fangs bared and his eyes were a deep red. He had no sense of control and fled from the room. Finding a servant in the nearby hallway, he ripped the poor man's throat into shreds and devoured his life in a single moment.

The servant was dead before Eliza could control Marcus. But lucky for her, another vampire entered the estate. Marcus turned his head because he could sense the stranger. Nostrils flaring, he dove for the man. But this man was too quick. Raising his hand in mid-air, he made a motion to squeeze his fist together, as if he had Marcus's neck between his fingers to strangle him.

"STOPPEN," commanded the old vampire. His voice was stern and sent fear into Marcus. Marcus lunged at the old man, but before he could come within an arm's reach, the vampire motioned his hand and Marcus was thrown across the room and into the wall. He fell to the floor and remained there, crumpled and broken.

"You will obey your maker Eliza, newborn. You will control that hunger of yours. You are essential to the Prophecy, and I serve the Avalani. You have purpose. Now, clean yourself up and obey." With that said, the old vampire left Marcus to his maker and retired to a room upstairs.

Marcus, still broken and breathing hard, asked, "What did you do to me?"

Eliza smiled and stroked his hair. "I simply gave you purpose. You were chosen to help mark the way. I am just a servant to our race. And now so are you." She left him to his thoughts to change her dress.

Marcus lay on the floor until she returned.

***

Eliza pulled him to his feet. She felt that it was time to pull him together and teach him what being a vampire meant. Thinking long and hard about how to do this, she knew it would be a challenge. She had never made a new vampire before, as she was a young vampire herself. The old vampire upstairs was her maker.

"Pull yourself together. We are going out on the town tonight."

Eliza could sense Marcus following her out the front door and towards the carriage. The horses were black as night and the carriage was a deep, dark red, almost matching the blood that he had drank from the gold cup. The ornate designs of the carriage were very elaborate and exquisite. Inside, the seat cushions were a velvet plush and definitely soft to the touch. Eliza made herself comfortable in the carriage and tapped her hand to the seat next to her. Gulping, he climbed into the carriage and sat on the opposite side to her. He looked afraid and confused.

The carriage pulled away as soon as he closed the door. The horses were trotting and soon they started going faster and faster. Eliza looked out at the night and smiled eerily.

***

Marcus did not like her smile nor her laughter, but he remained quiet. He, too, began looking out the window, and started thinking about what was happening to him. He had always heard the stories about the blood drinkers and thought they were just tales to scare people, but now he felt that he was one of them...one of those hated monsters that would drink the life of people just to feed.

Deep down, anger was boiling inside him, a rage that would not keep quiet. And there was something else. He looked at the mark of the vampire that was on his flesh. But there was another mark that only he could see.

Compelled to speak to her, he muscled up the courage to do so. *"¿Qué son esas marcas que me diste?"* Eliza said nothing to her charge, only smiled. Marcus waited but received no answer. He was getting furious at her treatment of him.

Finally, the carriage stopped and the door opened. A wanderer, shackled and chained, was thrown into the carriage by Eliza's driver. He looked haggard, though something was clear in his eyes. It was fear. On the man's right hand, a mark showed true...the mark of the witches. He tried to hide his hand but Marcus caught a glimpse of it, and soon his interest was sparked. Deep down, Marcus felt that he knew this man.

"¿Cuál es esa marca?" said Marcus, staring straight into the man's soul.

The frightened man covered his mark but spoke in plain English. "This is the mark of the witches.

You are a cold, dead blood drinker. Your path is unclean."

Marcus spoke in English, though he wasn't quite sure how he knew the language. "I am the cursed one from this wench. I have a hunger that she will not feed. I will drink from you, witch, but not until you tell me why I feel like I know you."

"You don't know me, but we are linked, young one. There is a prophecy, and I'll bet that red haired maiden sitting there hasn't told you a thing. That's why her servants captured me. Not only for you to feed, but for me to tell you about the other mark, the mark that is not visible to the eyes of others, but only to you at this moment in time."

"Tell me the prophecy." Marcus's voice boomed loudly inside the carriage.

"It begins with the Dark Man and a chosen witch of my bloodline some time ago. Through their love and binding, a fate is determined but no one knows of it. The story is passed through stories, words. There are no records of this love. If my bloodline continues, there will be born the most powerful witch the world will ever know. Her mark will score the flesh of the one who will be her consort. His love for her will prove merciless. Through them, a scepter will be created…an instrument for the queen, to be used at her will. If you see the mark of the witch, then you are the consort. But you will also become brother to another, who will be bound to the queen. We have waited a long time for the rebirth of the queen, the scepter, and the most powerful witch of my bloodline.

"Another witch will come in time, also of my bloodline. She will be that powerful witch's ally and enemy. You will come to know her by a special birthmark. You may feed off me, but in order to yield yourself to the Prophecy, you must let my bloodline continue. My children must be spared of what you will become. I am prepared to serve the Prophecy. But, in return, you must journey through the violence, the deaths, on your own; to find your way to this love, this prophecy. It is foretold that a man will bind himself with the most powerful witch to purify the strength of the Prophecy." And with that, the man said a chant of mercy in barely an audible whisper, and surrendered himself to Marcus.

Marcus saw the artery on the side of his neck and savagely tore into his flesh, drank the blood of the witch, and unknowingly moved the Prophecy forward. The man screamed and then silence filled the carriage. Blood stained the walls, Marcus, and Eliza's dress.

Eliza continued to look towards the night sky and Marcus felt that she was lost somewhere else because she was not feeding. Eliza still didn't say a word and that was disturbing to Marcus, but he didn't care at that point. Something had awakened inside him, and no one would understand what that was.

BARB JONES

CHAPTER THREE

Eliza and Marcus roamed the streets of the town. It was time Eliza taught him how to feed properly without destruction. But what she had seen in the carriage terrified her. She knew that Kabos had been stern about finding the boy and training him. But what else did he know? Gathering her skirts in her hands, she moved forward and prompted Marcus to follow her.

"Marcus, the first thing about feeding is that we drink blood, sometimes we kill. But we don't have to rip their bodies apart. You must show restraint and control. You can even compel the food to forget what they experienced to make it easier. But, Marcus, control is the key. You simply drink enough to satiate your hunger, but no more. We don't need any more newborns until Kabos is ready for a bigger family. He's your grandsire now. Learn, my son."

She noticed someone walking towards them, alone—a young woman, but no ordinary woman. Sniffing the air, Eliza smelled the stench of unclean sex, many men, and more. She was a prostitute. But nevertheless, this woman would satisfy Marcus.

"Go to the woman. Entice her, call her to you. Every vampire has a...well, a certain magnetism, and yours, dear boy, is your sex appeal...innocent looking, sexy...and you will learn to have an appetite for the other sex. Now, entice the bitch."

***

Marcus went to approach the woman, but somehow, during his transformation from man to vampire, he had also become clumsy. He stumbled on the cobblestones and fell. The young prostitute ran to him to see if he was alright. She spoke Spanish, and for that he was relieved. He was able to understand her and not the English that Eliza was speaking. He had known some English before, but because of the transformation, he understood when she spoke to him but was not able to speak the language.

"Estimado señor. ¿Está herido?" asked the prostitute. She may have sold her body to many men, and by the looks of it was old for the profession, but she was beautiful, with raven hair that fell to her shoulders, thick red lips that matched the color of wine, and pale skin that glowed in the moonlight. Her dress was not modest by any stretch of the imagination. Marcus assumed that she had just finished with a paying client.

Marcus looked up at her with a pained look in his eyes. He raised himself onto his elbow, staring directly into her eyes. He spoke to her in Spanish, unaware that he was also familiar with this language.

"*Perdóneme, señora, debo haber torcido el tobillo. Pero soy yo el que debe preguntar si está bien estar sin vigilancia en la noche. ¿Dónde está su escolta? Déjame cerca que el hombre falta a dejar una bella dama desatendida.*" (Translation: Pardon me, ma'am, I must have twisted my ankle. But it is I who must ask if you are all right, being unchaperoned in the night. Where is your escort? Let me near that foul man to leave a beautiful lady unattended.)

The prostitute, clearly shocked that Marcus did not recognize her profession, simply smiled and bent down to help him. She reached down towards his ankle, and before she could lift up his trousers leg to make sure he wasn't bleeding, he managed to pin her down and inhumanly sundered her throat from the rest of her body. There was no time for the woman to scream. Blood spewed from her neck and filled Marcus's mouth with as much as he was able to drink. His mouth did not leave her flesh until every drop of the red liquid was drained. Marcus finally stood above the dead woman, licked his lips, and stepped right over her. He did not care if his boot crushed her hand or not, she was already dead. His hunger still not satisfied, he moved past Eliza, searching for more victims.

Finding more victims to feed on, he left a line of bodies along the streets. Eliza could not keep up with him, and he noticed she pulled more and more away from him. Suddenly, as he was about to drink on the ninth body, thoughts entered his mind.

You must return to the estate before sunrise or you will burn. I have already left because I could not watch the destruction or terror that you started.

Obeying his master, he wandered the winding roads that took him away from the town and back to the estate. Staggering through the front doors, he collapsed to the floor as the sun's rays were rising in the east. The servants quickly closed the doors and drew the draperies closed. Two strong men hoisted Marcus to his feet and helped him into his bed, and left him in the dark room to slumber. Try as he might, he couldn't keep his eyes open and slept through the day.

***

Eliza entered the room and found Marcus asleep, still wearing the blood stained clothes from the night before. She thought about what it meant to be a newborn and tried to remember what it had felt like. Recalling her life as a newborn, she remembered how Kabos had saved her from her maker. Another newborn had turned her, and died a very short time later. Kabos found her and took her to Flanders, and taught her the ways of the vampire. Part of what she learned was the Prophecy...more importantly, the Blood Prophecy. A Prophecy that spanned many lifetimes and told the story of an important female vampire–known as the queen–and how her purpose was to save the wolves, the witches, and the vampires. All three races would be united and free under her domain was how Eliza understood it. But they must find these key individuals in order to fulfill the Prophecy. She also knew that there were some prepared to destroy the Prophecy.

A puzzling question to her was how Marcus fit in. He was uncontrollable, untamable, yet sensitive and loving. Could he be taught to curb his heightened senses?

Eliza opened the draperies to let the night in. After all, they were creatures of the night and it was time to waken. Marcus started to stir but he didn't open his eyes. His talons were stretched outward and his body writhed under the covers. Twisting and turning, he was mumbling in his sleep. Furious with her newborn, she pulled back the covers and slapped him across the face. With his eyes still closed, his fangs appeared and his nostrils flared.

"I dare you, boy, to hurt me. Tonight you will learn to control your hunger, your rage, and more. We do not feed tonight, but you will listen to me. If not me, then Kabos."

Marcus stirred even more but did not wake. Instead, he rolled over and started to snore.

She gave him another slap to his face, and this time his right hand reached for her neck. Before his fingers could close around her throat, she elbowed him directly in the face.

"You will show obedience, brute. I am your maker."

***

Marcus exhaled deeply, and not long after he let out a piercing scream. His flesh began to burn inexplicably. Eliza was not doing this to him, nor was Kabos; he sensed that. His eyes turned from their dark shade to a golden yellow. Nostrils blazing with deep breaths, Marcus could no longer control his person. A voice erupted from him, speaking aloud.

"This vessel is the chosen consort. He is marked by the witches but is now marked by the seers. Through his loins comes the child of joining, but it will be an eternity of hell that he will endure. His rage must consume him to the point where he will learn love. Free him of his bonds and return him to us. The Avalani are the chosen kindred who rule and will be obeyed."

Marcus coughed and the smell of burning flesh left the room. There was no new mark that he or Eliza could see. Having heard the words that were spoken, Eliza turned and left the room, leaving him alone once more.

CHAPTER FOUR

Kabos listened to the story Eliza had just finished. He nodded his head in acquiescence and rubbed his hand under his chin. "Your brother, Eliza, is the one whose fate is tied to the queen. This one newborn is also part of the Prophecy. That has been determined by the seers. I leave him to you to either teach him the ways or let him go into the world. I must return to Michael and prepare him.

I have more knowledge of the Prophecy than any other vampire, and that secret will remain between you and me, my sweet daughter. But know this...Michael and the newborn cannot meet until the time is right. I will be in touch."

Eliza looked at him with eyes full of questions, but Kabos remained quiet. He thought for a moment about changing his mind and staying with her because this was her first newborn, but he recalled the words from the Avalani. The Prophecy's players must all come together on their own in order to begin.

***

Eliza didn't understand what Kabos was doing, but she knew better than to pester him with questions. Running her right hand over her left arm, she smiled and acknowledged his words. "Goodbye, Father. I will do as you wish. Let's not make it too long before we meet again. Tell my brother I wish him well."

With that said, she turned on her heels and left. Returning to Marcus's room, she found him pacing the floor in a fit of rage. Drinking goblets, vases, and more were thrown all across the room, shattered and in pieces. The draperies were in shreds and a servant cowered in the corner. The man had wet himself for fear of dying. He was always a good servant, Eliza realized. Another man was next to him, broken and dead. His head was torn from his body and his blood spilled onto the floor. It looked like this man had been carrying a tray with wine before Marcus took his life.

"Get up, Gregory. Go and clean yourself. I will take over. Tell no one to enter this room unless I bid it. Leave the body for now."

Eliza hoisted her skirts and carefully stepped over the body, and watched Marcus as she heard the servant leave. Sighing heavily, she spoke to her newborn in an old tongue. Upon hearing the words, Marcus turned and dropped his hands to his sides. He was listening and had no choice but to obey. Obedience was what she demanded in the old tongue.

"I am your master. I know you will love me, all men love me. That is my ability. But, I must send you away. I have to send you out into the mortal world, untaught and without the knowledge of survival. I wish I didn't have to, but the words in the Prophecy speak otherwise. You must rage before you can be taught by another. My part in this Prophecy is now complete. Leave me, Marcus, leave me now. We will not meet again."

***

Marcus changed his clothes and gathered his courage to speak against his master. Eyes on fire, his voice deep and hardened, he came no less than three inches from her face. Breathing hard and fast, he told her, "You do not control me, master or not. There is something inside me that hates you with a burning passion that I can't control. I did not ask for this, wench. You did this to me. You turned me into a monster that I despise. It is not right and just that I am what I am. Prophecy or not, I am not your pawn." Once those words were spoken, his eyes turned red and he bit into her neck. "Touch me again, bitch, or command me, and I will hunt you down and kill you."

Marcus then fled the room, leaving the estate behind, and began his own journey.

CHAPTER FIVE

It had been three months since that night he'd left Eliza. All this time, Marcus had wandered the country killing and destroying. Senses heightened with a rage that would not end, Marcus was the reason why townspeople hid inside their homes once the sun set. Children could no longer play outside and laugh with others, and women were afraid to socialize or attend church. Though the towns were full of God-fearing people, they took to honoring Sunday services in their homes, avoided the social functions, and stayed locked indoors.

Night after night bodies were lined up along the pathways. Flies were buzzing around the dead folk, and the constable couldn't understand what was happening to the women in the town. Marcus roamed the nights as did some of the men, searching for the ruthless killers. Then, slowly he would prey upon the women that were not afraid to be in the open. Drinking the blood and dismembering the bodies, Marcus left a cold trail of vile wretchedness and carnage in his path.

Finally, he came upon an old church in one of the towns he

encompassed. Time was passing this church by. No longer holding any evidence that people once worshipped there, he was able to pass onto the grounds, but he could not enter the building. A crotchety old man came around the corner, waving his cane at Marcus. He could smell the old man and the stench of death that surrounded his body.

"Old man, what do you want?" shouted Marcus.

"You, you filth. You are one of the cold ones. Leave this town. I am Bertrund, Seer of the Clan. But, you are different. There's something about you. Come closer, old one."

Marcus was in disbelief that the old man knew what he was, and the fact that he was learning on his own how to survive as a vampire disturbed him. He came as close as he could, because as he was ready to take one more step towards the old man, Marcus could not raise his foot. Some force was preventing his foot from being lifted. There he stood, waiting. The old man approached, but stopped before getting too close to him.

"You are a newborn, made not too long ago. You smell of the one who is a friend to our dear Besnik. You also smell as if you don't belong in this world. Sit, my boy. Sit and listen to a story."

Marcus was unsure, but he remembered that he was a vampire and could devour this old man in one bite if he became cross. He sat down on the damp earth and listened to the tale.

"We seers have a tale, and an interest in the oldest Prophecy known to man. It is something, you could say, that has been handed down for many centuries. Listen carefully, because it is not written down in one place. I will tell you the story and then I will hide it from your mind until you are ready, young friend. It has many parts, and different races own a portion of the Prophecy. It is written that a queen of your kind loved the werewolves as much as she loved your race, the blood drinkers. She believed that the two races could live in unification and purity, even to the point where they could come together as husband and wife.

"She was betrothed and married to the king...the king of the *strigoi*, who himself was created from the original one of your kind. I believe your race goes by the word vampire, but we seers call you the *strigoi*. She fell in love with the *varcolac*, what you refer to as werewolves. She and their alpha were bound by a love as thick as the stars in the night sky. But, the king was a vile and ruthless ruler who demanded that the *varcolac* serve your kind for all days. From the fire she was born, and grew with power and strength. All who knew her loved her. But the king managed to destroy her and her *varcolac*. The Prophecy was born because that was the night of the Blood Moon. She will rise once more, and so will her *varcolac*. She will be the instrument of the Prophecy, and her fate will be decided by the Blood Moon's rising. The seers will come to her aid, but at a price that is not known yet. Her debt will be paid when the Blood Moon rises for the third time in the world.

"Her blood will be spilled and her justice unveiled. But she will provide unification with a child.

"So, my young friend, I see the hidden mark inside you. You are part of the Prophecy. You must yield your soul to a powerful one and your rage will be your salvation. Your heart will become pure once you forsake all others for the powerful one. Through her, your salvation will be born. You must pay the price to the Prophecy as foretold by the seers over the years. You must rage before you can be tamed. You will be full of hatred until you are loved."

Marcus remained quiet but was confused by the old man's words. The old man stepped back from him and drew a circle in the earth. He used his walking stick to draw a triangle in the center of the circle. An eye filled the triangle by the time he was done drawing in the earth. "This is the symbol of the seers. Memorize this symbol, because it will guide you to another blood drinker. Together you become formidable. But first, you will not remember until it's time." He grabbed some dirt from the middle of the symbol and blew it onto Marcus.

With that said, the old man disappeared in the same direction from which he had come. Marcus was left alone in the old churchyard. A burning sensation erupted from his side, but there was no mark. He was left wondering what he was doing sitting there when he had to feed. He needed blood.

His mind weak and confused, he stood up and went to search for food. He found sheep nearby and the humans that tended to them. Savagely he tore into the shepherds' bodies and drained them completely. He managed to feed on both men in a matter of seconds, while their spilled blood covered the white fur of the sheep. Knowing that sun would rise soon, he fled to the confines of an old structure to sleep.

CHAPTER SIX

When he awoke, Marcus continued his path of rage and hatred. However, having been gone all this time from family and friends, he was lonely. He wanted to see his friends and he missed his mother greatly. But that loneliness soon dissipated, and again rage consumed his being.

Looking out at the countryside, he could smell the winery. The fresh scent of wine filled him, and he knew if there was fresh wine, there was fresh blood. He continued to let the hatred and rage guide him forward.

There was not enough blood to keep him sustained. It wasn't that he was hungry...he was enjoying the killing, the hunting, and the look of fear in their eyes as he showed them what he truly was. But no matter how much he tried, he couldn't forget about Eliza...those perfect lips, her hair, shapely hips, and a bosom that was captivating. Though he didn't really know her well, he loved the bloodletting. His manly parts started to bulge as thoughts of her filled his mind. The next moment his head was throbbing.

Marcus, Marcus.

It sounded like her voice. Eliza. But it was in his head. It was all he heard.

Marcus.

Again, he didn't respond. He didn't know what this was.

MARCUS!

The shrill female voice in his head sent a painful tingling sensation down his arms and to his fingertips. It also sent his body reeling backwards when he lost his balance.

Yes? He finally answered as he tried to regain control of his functions.

You were thinking of me. We are connected. I am your sire. When you long for me, I can feel it. We are not meant to be together. The path that is chosen for you was set before we met.

You must follow the path as you discover it.

I don't know what you are talking about. All I know is that I am always hungry and I don't care what happens. You have forsaken me for some stupid legend – oh, excuse me, prophecy – that means shit to me. We should be bloodletting right now. That is all I know from you.

Follow the marks of the prophecy. They will guide you to your purpose. If you want me, you will need to find me. But I will not interfere with your destiny.

This infuriated Marcus and brought him once more into a fit of hatred. He loathed that beautiful woman, yet he wanted her at the same time.

***

From a distance she was able to watch him...the newborn vampire that the heavens had told her about. She was not another vampire, she was not a witch, and she was not a seer. Instead, her name was Azraela, keeper of the Prophecy. No one knew she watched over them, as her body was translucent. It was her duty to make sure that those chosen would find their path according to the Prophecy.

This young one was special. His destiny was marked and created. She smiled at the mere thought that his anger would one day become his ally and his strength. Azraela looked up to the heavens and smiled lovingly at the clouds that floated above.

A carriage was moving past her and towards Marcus. She knew what would happen if he just yielded himself. Two young women were in the carriage with a driver on the outside. The women were finely dressed and the carriage was decorated lavishly. She waited and watched carefully, but what she saw infuriated her. The newborn was supposed to launch a carnage attack on the women, but instead he hung his head down and continued walking past the moving carriage.

In order for him to learn obedience and loyalty, he needed to complete his transformation.

Damn fool. I must initiate something else to move him along. He needs to be vulnerable and desperate in order to be taught.

***

Marcus continued past the carriage. The smell of human blood was simply delicious and inviting, but having just learned that Eliza could speak to him in his head depressed him. If he wanted her, he needed to find her. Did she think of him as her lapdog? Marcus was disgusted at that thought and all thirst for blood left him. He was becoming a broken vampire.

In silence, he sent his thoughts to Eliza.

I am assuming that I have the unfortunate experience to only talk to you this way, dear Eliza. Or shall I call you my mother? Do you think that the only way I can find peace is your way? Then, you don't know me well enough, do you? You come to me needing to start a so-called prophecy, or story as you put it. I am not your plaything. You will be my plaything when I find you, dear Eliza. Be forewarned.

With lightning speed Marcus was through the countryside and on his way to Eliza's estate. He found the estate easily enough, but once he crossed through the gates, he saw that the grass was overgrown with weeds, the front doors were off their hinges, and signs of a fire that had spread through the home were evident. Draperies were torn to shreds and grayish soot lined the floors, both upstairs and downstairs. On the front hallway niche a broken candelabra remained, but on the wall behind was a strange symbol. It looked like an upside down V with a circle above it. He did not remember seeing this before.

Marcus explored the estate but found no signs of living servants or Eliza. She had not mentioned that she was no longer on the estate when she communicated with him.

Eliza, you must still be alive, and by the looks of your estate, you barely escaped. I will find you. Let me come to you.

Before Eliza could answer him, Marcus's flesh burned once more and he dropped to the ground writhing in pain. As he screamed, a man appeared from the shadows and stood over him. Through the screams, Marcus opened his eyes and saw the dark colored shoes and continued to look up. He wanted to know who this man was. When his eyes found the man's face, he saw a scar on his cheek. It matched the mark on the wall.

"Foolish vampire. Don't you know who I am?" he said in a deep, hoarse voice. With his free hand, he lowered his hat to cover his eyes more.

"N...no."

"I am Valentine, hunter of the blood drinkers...better known as vampires. But don't worry, newborn. Yes, I can smell the fresh make on you. I don't want you, at least not yet. I need you to connect with who you are. I want the one who made you."

Then, before Marcus could answer, the hunter's other hand raised from his side and an arrow was shot. The arrow landed near Marcus's heart and his head fell back; he was out cold.

***

Valentine looked over his prey and studied him. He had been fully aware of the Prophecy since the time his beloved wife was taken from him. He preferred his broadsword but settled at times for his bow and arrow. The arrow proved to be more efficient against the vampires. His dark coat was damp and full of soot, but nevertheless, he kept it on as he kicked the vampire.

Damn newborn. He doesn't even know how he fits in this, he thought silently.

He laughed once more as he left the estate in search of this newborn's maker, Eliza.

***

Eliza was always his target but he was too late, because he had wanted to prevent this newborn's "birth."

BARB JONES

Chapter Seven

Eliza roamed the streets in search of a new place of shelter. This was most unusual for a woman of her status. A man approached her and saw that she needed help. "*Señora, ¿Necessitas ayuda?*" His smile was gentle and kind...it reminded her of Kabos. The man reached for her and she smiled back. His eyes showed compassion and longing. She grasped his hand and told him what happened...not the full truth, but enough to gain his sympathy; her estate caught fire and she barely got out alive. He listened and offered her a seat in his store. Eliza followed and enjoyed a cup of tea with him.

He sipped the tea while she played with the spoon, hoping he did not notice that she didn't take a drink.

"Sir, I speak English. Yes?"

"Ah, English. Of course. I am fluent in both."

"Thank you for your kindness. I am forever flattered by it," she said as she smiled sheepishly at him. He did not respond for a few moments. The silence was awkward. Because it was, Eliza took a sip of the tea. Deep inside, her body was fighting the tea but her mind was strong. Kabos had taught her that she needed to appear to fit in with the humans.

"It's getting late, sir. I must get ready to leave, but I'm so tired. I can't move...."

Before she could finish her sentence, Eliza fell back in the chair, conscious, but unable to move or speak.

***

Brohman, the nice shopkeeper, wasn't so nice after all. He had kept the marking of his clan covered so that Eliza would not see it. He was a seer, a member of the Romani gypsy clan that had been guarding the Prophecy for a very long time. People thought he was a strange man, not quite scary but eccentric. He had peculiar ways about him that made them leave him alone, which suited Brohman just fine.

He changed the sign on his shop to read Closed. No need for inquisitive people to disturb him. Brohman sat down and looked at his captive. There was fear in her eyes, but there was also determination. Stroking her cheek with his hand softly, he began to chant. Her body resisted at first, but then it became more and more relaxed.

"Beautiful *strigoi*. Soft and tender. You run from what you fear. I shall help you, *strigoi*."

His captive said nothing but the look in her eyes told him that she did not understand her fate. Brohman chuckled to himself as he turned to leave her for just a moment. He needed to kindle the fire to keep his store warm.

When he returned, he found her exactly where he'd left her. After all, where would she go?

"*Strigoi*, you will not recall what happened. The hour of your death is not yet come. You must find the witch's consort, your newborn. He is searching for you. My clan is bound to him and others. But, it is you that he seeks. The *vânător*, what you call hunter, is searching for you. You are the key to making this newborn, and you succeeded. But let me share with you what I see. *Strigoi*, you will then understand.

"You will eventually die by the *vânător*, but not tomorrow or the day after the morrow. The newborn needs you. You need him. Souls connected, but not as lovers. He needs to learn how to kill in order to learn how to love. Teach him and fulfill your purpose. You need to learn anger in order to teach him. This dust I blow on you will help you. If you don't, the *vânător* will find you because that is your destiny. Your purpose. Other than that, you are a useless *strigoi*. And the one who knows us knows this. Your father. My friend, Kabos."

With that Brohman repeated the chant, blew the dust on her, and then she was free. Before he could say anything else to her, she leapt from the chair, sunk her teeth into him, and started to drink from him. Brohman fell to the floor, unconscious and barely breathing, Eliza looked at him and licked the blood from her lips with a flick of her tongue.

***

Eliza, the once so sweet and smiling vampire, was no more. She managed to find a mirror and looked at herself closely. Her hair was in disarray and her makeup was smeared. She definitely did not look the part of a lady by any stretch of the imagination. She retreated and walked over the seer and into his back room. Surely he must have a change of clothes somewhere, or even facilities for a lady to wash and clean herself.

She was finally clean and did not show the wear and tear on her person like before. Bending down, Eliza grabbed his wrists and started walking backwards, with Brohman's body dragging on the floor. Best to keep him hidden. Because she was feeling weak, she decided that an almost dead man was just as tasty as a live man. Her fangs became elongated and she drank from him once more. With each drop of blood, she began to feel more alive. Eliza found a cloth and patted any remnants of blood from her face.

Using her mind, she reached for Marcus. For some reason she could not explain, she didn't feel the need to abandon him as she had before. She needed him and reached out.

Marcus, sweet lamb. Come to me as I am your maker. I will teach you.

Eliza waited. It didn't take long for Marcus to arrive at the store once she called. The wait was mere minutes because they were, as Brohman had put it, *strigoi*. And *strigoi* fed on the blood of the living. The thought just made her smile.

Sensing Marcus at the door, she emerged from the back and opened it. He stood there, looking well-fed and content, yet angry after being separated for a few months. When she saw that he was still beautiful to look at, she felt the need to drag him inside, ravage him, and drink his blood while he drank hers. The thought became a reality as she grabbed his hands and began kissing him.

Her teeth sank into his bottom lip and a tiny dabble of blood reached her tongue. Her eyes turned red and she bit harder to drink more. Marcus returned the favor by biting back into her and letting the blood mix with his. As both vampires became consumed with bloodletting, Eliza quickened the pace. Her hands found his pants and ripped them off his hips. She stroked his body, and he responded by clasping the front of her dress and pulling the lacing apart with such passion that the dress could not be worn again.

Eliza felt his tongue flicker on her neck as he threw her to the floor. Bloodletting and sex were the beginning of their new life together.

CHAPTER EIGHT

Eliza and Marcus woke the next night, ready to create havoc on the innocent townspeople. Marcus finally felt that Eliza understood him and accepted him. The night before had been full of intensity and passion, and they had found a dark corner in the store to sleep through the daylight. Their appearances were now clean, and both looked the part of sophisticated shopkeepers now that they had disposed of the body.

Leaving the shop and making sure the sign read Closed, the young couple ventured out into the world.

After travelling for many days, feeding, sleeping, and bloodletting, they came across a nice provincial town. Not a soul knew who they were; not a memory stirred in the minds of men. This was a chance to start fresh. For all they knew, they were no longer in Flanders, Spain, or anywhere close. England was giving them a chance to begin anew.

A new start. A new chance to show the world who they really were. Marcus realized that during all their travels together, Eliza was his. She may have been the maker, but there was something new about her that allowed him to enjoy the viciousness of being a vampire.

As they settled into the new town, Marcus was realizing that pieces of his memory were not intact. He and Eliza spoke seldom of the night in which he was summoned back to her. But the one thing they shared was the knowledge of the same symbol...the symbol of the seers. This seemed to draw them closer to each other, while at the same time filled them with an uncontrollable lust for rage and hunger.

The English countryside was as beautiful at night as it was during the day. Both were so relieved to be in a town that provided a fresh start, but at a cost to the citizens. Every three nights bodies lined the haystacks on which the sheep were grazing. Shepherds never noticed the bodies that piled up at the haystacks simply because they were lazy and did not want to walk farther than they had to. The sheep never mutilated the bodies, and the stench seemed to absorb into the natural smell of the pasture. No one was the wiser.

In the village, people assumed that their neighbors were relocating due to the stressful times with the monarchy. Marcus and Eliza settled in perfectly as workers of the crown. They showed their loyalty to the monarchy by paying taxes, and Eliza chose to work diligently, though at night. Both were faithful to the community and attended evening socials, interacted with the others, and more. No one thought of them as different.

***

Eliza found herself amongst the women tending to their daily chores, although it was night. The men were always looking out for strange things at that time, so the women were alone.

"Mistress Eliza, what do you and Master Marcus think of our village since you moved in? It must be strange that so many of us prefer to work at night rather than the daytime," asked a homely looking mistress. She had always tried to befriend Eliza. She was pleasantly plump, had a crooked nose, and two beady-looking eyes, which made Eliza cringe. Dressed warmly though but not too finely, the woman was very modest looking to the eye. A small scar was on her shoulder that was not covered by her bodice.

"What is that scar from, may I ask?"

"Oh that. Not too long ago our village was infested by a pack of dogs or wolves. One never knows based on their size. I was scratched by one of them with its claws as it took a bite out of my leg. My late husband managed to shoot him before he himself was bitten and died of the bite." The mistress couldn't continue because tears welled up in her eyes.

Tenderness and softness for the woman overcame Eliza as she put her hands on the woman's shoulders. Eliza could feel that she was hurt and lonely for the only man she'd ever loved. Turning the woman to her and making sure that the others couldn't hear, she stared deeply into her eyes.

"You will always remember him, but starting today, you will live knowing that he loved you. You are not lonely anymore, but will surround yourself with friends who will love you. When you are ready, you will one day open your heart to another."

Eliza was surprised at the kindness towards this woman when just last night they had fed on some of their neighbors. Hunger began to emerge and she could feel herself losing control again. Politely excusing herself, Eliza left and found her way back to Marcus.

***

Time passed. Slowly Marcus was coming up on the first

anniversary of his being a vampire. Both he and Eliza fell into a routine. The villagers never suspected that they were the reasons why the town was falling into a shortage in regards to the population. Most felt that the economy and the rumors of King George III being crazy were the reasons why people left. Regardless, people took to their daily living and continued on.

Marcus's behavior was getting the best of him, and somehow Eliza was part of that. He didn't understand what had changed her, but it was not like the Eliza he knew. Ever since he had come to her after she summoned him, something wasn't right. She kept to herself but her teachings were more vicious and full of animosity than ever before. They didn't kiss any more, and Eliza never showed any signs of affection towards him. It was purely teacher-student in that regard.

Eliza came back to the cottage that they shared. She slammed the door shut and started shouting. Her hair was no longer wavy or full of life; in fact, it was a mass of tangles and her red lipstick smeared onto her cheek. Her dress was wet and she was breathing heavily. Her eyes showed fear and loathing.

"Marcus, we need to leave now. The village will know it is us, and we either have to kill them all or we leave. We are outnumbered, so leaving is the best choice."

Marcus did not respond to her. He was paralyzed at her behavior, watching her breathe heavily.

"Marcus, fool. Are you even listening to me?"

Finally he had the courage to speak. "Yes, we will leave. Let me get my things."

Before anything else could be said, the stinging of the strike from her hand brought him back to reality. He was shocked that Eliza slapped him, but he was not afraid of her. Over the months he had been learning secretly how to overcome the sire bond without her knowledge. And it was working. He had stopped drinking her blood for starters. He was waiting for her to share with him anything about her recent behavior, such as why she was as blood thirsty as he was. But she never did.

Instead she grabbed him by the throat and hurled him against the wall. His anger was beginning to boil, and looking at her made his skin crawl. A deep growl rose from his lips while his fangs protruded. As he hoisted himself to his feet, a sense of enmity came over him. He despised her and loved her at the same time. His sides began to ache and the smell of burning flesh became intense.

"Don't defy me, maker. I have had it with your damn secrets and your fucking lies. You weren't this way before, and this life is a complete and utter falsehood. I will take a fucking knife and stab you in the heart and twist it till I hear your bones crunch. And after that, I will take a stake and replace the knife with it. You won't know pain until I am done with you. You won't know if I will kill you today or tomorrow.

Or better yet, let me call upon the one you are so afraid of to kill you while I watch, you miserable filthy bitch."

Eliza's eyes showed fear and she ran to the window.

***

Eliza was afraid; not because of what Marcus had said, but because of what she saw outside. She saw villagers with torches marching in their direction, following him...the hunter. She remembered what Kabos told her of his name. Valentine.

"You want to kill me, fine. Kill me. But do it after we leave. I can't fail you. Let's go."

Marcus never responded, but because of his mood towards her, he followed her out the back and

they were never seen in that village
again.

CHAPTER NINE

It was finally 1794. Marcus and Eliza had spent the past year running from town to town, village to village. They never settled in a place for too long. However, this was not their normal feeding night. In fact, they had grown closer together despite Marcus's words on that dreadful night. Each morning when they would retire, Eliza wondered if she'd wake later that night. But she always did.

A knock on the door surprised them, but Eliza opened it and saw a stranger standing there dripping wet. She didn't even know that it was raining.

"Come inside. Let's get you out of those wet clothes."

"Thank you, madame. But first, where is your husband? I don't want to intrude or violate your, ah, safety."

Marcus suddenly appeared right behind Eliza and placed his arm around her waist. She moved a little closer to him, showing the stranger that he was going to be a formidable opponent if given the opportunity. The stranger recognized the signs.

He pulled back his sleeve and told them to look closely at his arm. Marcus moved around Eliza so he could take a closer look at his arm. His eyes narrowed, and what he saw surprised him. On the man's forearm a triangle with a golden eye stared straight back at him. Chills crept up and down his spine, but he couldn't say anything because Eliza interrupted his thoughts.

"I know that mark. You are a seer. What are you doing here? Our kinds do not speak to each other. That is the first rule that we learn." Eliza's fangs came out as her breathing got deeper.

With a free hand the stranger managed to blow something in their faces, and before anything else was said or done, Marcus could not move or speak. It seemed to him that Eliza was in the same predicament. Both fell to the cottage floor and looked up at the stranger.

The stranger stood over Marcus and started to chant something he didn't understand. He couldn't fight back, he couldn't resist, but what he felt instead made his insides feel like they were coming out of his body. A mark finally made its appearance but he couldn't see it, only feel the burning that he had come to know so well.

The stranger then moved to Eliza and Marcus worried what he would do. The stranger said a different chant over her. But she didn't move and no sound came from her.

***

Looking down at the two vampires, the stranger smiled. If only they knew what they needed to endure in order to become strong. His part in this was almost over, but not until he spoke to them. As he incanted another chant, the two vampires could speak but not move. He did not want to take a chance and be killed by these two.

The male vampire spoke. "What do you want with us, stranger? Why do you seek us out yet you do not kill us?" The female vampire said nothing.

"Foolish boy. Not all of our kind, the Romani, fear you or wish you harmed. I am of the elite group who protect and believe in the Prophecy. A long awaited revelation is coming in which there will be a time when all will find justice and unification; but only under the power of a queen. Your part is yet to come, but we needed to mold you into that vampire to be. Now that you know such violence, you are ready to find love. This one next to you, your maker. She must now teach you to love. From love, you must find truth. From truth, you must find conviction and purpose. Heed my words, young newborn. Your place in the Prophecy will be decided once you achieve those things and in that order."

The male vampire replied quietly. "I understand. But whatever my innocence cost me, I know that I must serve."

The stranger took his leave, and once he left the cottage he knew that the two vampires' ability to move returned.

***

Marcus took notice of the spoken words and looked at Eliza. Instead of feeling furious with her as he had earlier, he felt more compassion and feeling toward her. As soon as the stranger left, the loathing and vile behavior left Marcus. He wondered if the same had happened for Eliza.

Looking at her, he saw her facial features change from hardness to a soft tenderness. Her eyes were no longer narrow, but full of wonder and life, and her lips returned to their soft fullness. Her breathing became steady once more. She started to sit up.

He took her at the crook of her elbow and helped her to her feet. His hands brushed some loose strands of hair from her face, and cupping her chin in his hand, he kissed her with emotion. Her mouth responded by opening and allowing him to feel her tongue. It was just a kiss, but a loving one.

Marcus hoisted her into his arms and carried her to the bedroom that they shared. But once he saw the walls stained with dark traces of old blood, he left her on the bed and went to clean the walls. There would be no horrifying reminders of the past.

***

Eliza found herself in a much calmer state than before. In fact, she appreciated that he was cleaning the walls. Silence filled her. The poor men and women that fed them unwillingly had been splattered on the walls with such desire at that time. Now grief consumed her. Grief for her behavior in the past. She felt the need to speak to Kabos, but remembered his words. She needed to teach Marcus.

.

CHAPTER TEN

Marcus sat Eliza up, who appeared to be more in shock than anything else. Eliza used mind speech to communicate with him.

I don't remember anything. Did we have a fainting spell?

He, of course, remembered all the events that had led up to this night. All the carnage, savagery, debauchery, Marcus remembered it all. There was no turning back from his period as the vile creature he had become. But having heard the stranger's words, he took a long look at Eliza. She appeared to him to look naïve, innocent, and was the most beautiful woman he had seen in many years. He looked at her longingly and with compassion.

Eliza turned to him and for once in a very long time, her eyes were full of love and wonder. Remembering what Kabos had wanted for Marcus, it was now her duty to teach him the ways. Feelings of lust stirred in her loins and made her feel warm. She could smell her body's reaction to the thought of taking him in her arms and moving her body in sync with his. As she was getting ready to entice Marcus into bed and to leave the cleaning till later, she noticed that he had already left to refill the bucket with warm water.

She stayed on the bed but removed her clothes in hopes of attracting Marcus to her. Her back was arched and poised in a way that would let him know that she wanted him. Her body was his invitation to forgiveness, and hopes that they could restore what had been started before he went his own way.

***

Marcus found her and immediately dropped the bucket of sudsy water. Climbing on top, he found her ready for him. Her nipples were already hardened and her body was wet. She did not need the touch of his fingers or tongue between her legs to get her ready. Sliding himself in between her legs, his body began to move with hers. They were together.

Finally, after both came with heat and passion, he lay down next to her and stared at the roof of the cottage, then closed his eyes and waited for someone to speak. He was secretly hoping that she would talk about this Prophecy and why he was so important to it. As if she was reading his mind, she began to speak.

"Marcus, it is time we talked. I mean *really* talked. Kabos, my father, isn't really my maker. My maker died a short time after I was made and Kabos rescued me. He taught me the ways that every one of our kind needs to know. Through him, I learned about the Avalani, the Covenant, the Prophecy, all this chaos. It is said that the one who has a secret marking will be born. You have that secret marking. You are destined for greatness that is yet to come. Your marking will be visible when you have found your true mate. Till then, I will teach you the true way you need to follow. We can be lovers in the meantime, too. After all, we move rather nicely together, don't you think?"

"Yes, we do. In order for me to learn from you, don't we need to talk about the things I did? What I became once I left you?"

"There will be plenty of time for that. Just like there is plenty of time to clean the cottage. But now, this is the time to play. Come play with me, I command it."

Marcus realized the tone and was forced to obey his maker. They played in the bed once more.

***

Marcus and Eliza realized that it was time to move on. They were no longer safe where they were. Having a few essentials packed and ready to go, the two set out to find their next home. Little did they know that members of the Avalani were all around them. In fact, Marcus and Eliza only saw villagers, and after some time and distance, the village was nothing but a memory.

Days and weeks passed. Finally, they began to reach a point in their travels where weariness took over. They needed to find a home once more.

A dwelling called out to them by being isolated from neighbors or anyone else. It was perfectly inviting and waiting for them to settle in. They approached the little cottage and immediately moved in.

CHAPTER ELEVEN

Marcus settled into a routine and waited for the right moment to ask Eliza about the Prophecy. It was one of those cold nights in which they did not need to feed, but sat around the fire pretending to be a normal young couple. For the past several months they had fed every three nights, and usually on the animals in the countryside. They couldn't bring themselves to feed on men at the moment.

Using the stick to stir and awaken the fire in the earth, Marcus had begun to ask Eliza about the origins of the Prophecy when she interrupted his questions. She motioned for him to sit and he found a chair and sat. The room was silent.

Eliza found a broom and started sweeping while she began to tell the story as she had learned it from Kabos.

"We were known in years past by many different names. The cold ones, blood drinkers, *strigoi*, *vampyr*, and more. Our nature is not that different from the nature of our prey, except that we don't eat food anymore. We can only survive with the drink of blood. People have come to fear us, creating legends for something that they do not yet understand. But we exist.

"Long before all that there was a beautiful queen. I can't remember all the details about her, but she was friendly with the slaves we kept. Filthy smelling dogs is what we called them, but today they are known as werewolves. She believed in equality for their kind and ours. But the king vowed to kill her and he did. The Prophecy will bring her back to stop the war between our kinds and others.

"See, it's not a fancy tale. I can't tell it the way Kabos did with the voices, the translations, and hand gestures," she said, giggling.

Marcus knew that it felt good to hear her laugh and smile, as when he had first met her. She looked so beautiful sweeping the floor in the candlelight. There were no other sounds in the cottage except for them and the crackling of the fire to keep them warm. He realized that they had travelled great distances since they'd first met, and that they knew no boundaries. The sudden realization that he loved her hit Marcus, but his instincts told him that she wasn't the one meant for him. She was so breathtaking and stunning in her looks. He wondered how she felt about him since she'd made him.

"I understand why the Prophecy is so important, but I don't understand why me."

Eliza stopped sweeping and approached him. She sat herself in his lap and spoke once more.

"Dear Marcus, do you know anything of your family history?"

As long as Marcus could remember he had been an orphan, because his family could not feed another babe. He was left at the clockmaker's doorstep and was taken in by the man and his wife. He grew up loving them, but was told the truth when he became of age to understand. His eyes softened as he recalled the old clockmaker fondly.

Sadly, he shook his head in answer to Eliza's question.

"Well, there is more in the Prophecy that announces why certain ones are chosen for this. There's something in your familial history that makes you a pawn in the Prophecy. Discover that and you will understand why it is you. Alas, that is all I can tell you, because that is all I know."

Marcus touched her hand and then her cheek. Reaching for her hand once more, he held it and kissed it lovingly. He waited a bit before speaking to her again. "I'm sorry, this is too much for me. I'm going out to hunt. I hope you will be here when I come back. I will return before the sun rises."

***

Eliza knew that he must be feeling overwhelmed with the news of how he was part of this thing, as she liked to reference the Prophecy. If only she could remember how Kabos told the tale to her, it might have been better. But she didn't feel the need to talk about the Avalani, that horrible group her father had a part in. Something inside her told her that not all of them could be trusted. Her father, Kabos, yes, but not the rest. Not that sneaky bastard, Gerard. He was a fat, conniving, and vicious vampire. There was always something sinister in his eyes.

Watching Marcus leave was the hardest thing she had to do, but she knew he would come back to her. He said he would. Maybe he needed time to understand what she had told him, and now, to learn to deal with the fact that he knew nothing of his family heritage and legacy. All she understood was that this was a key part to understanding how he fit in. She continued to sweep the cottage clean and when that was done, the candles were blown out, all but one. One candle remained in the window to guide him home to her.

***

He wasn't in the mood to hunt. Marcus just needed to take a walk to clear his mind after the story Eliza had revealed to him. He wanted so badly to find the truth, now more than ever. Where did he come from? Why was he so important? Continuing his walk in circles, Marcus ignored the cool breeze that touched him. There was something different about this night, unlike the other nights that had come before.

Marcus turned up the collar on his coat and looked around. He decided to head back to the cottage where Eliza was waiting. Before he had taken three steps forward, his side began to sting, and something appeared...a circle with lines through it. It was strange, but it seared his skin and reminded him of his making. He clenched his teeth as his body hovered forward, and he began to writhe in pain, excruciating pain.

Then the pain stopped, and the mark disappeared.

He knew what he had to do. He returned to the cottage where Eliza waited for him.

"Eliza! Eliza!"

"I'm here, Marcus. Sit down. You brought the cold in from the outside." Eliza brought a blanket and covered his shoulders with it. On the table she sat a cup of brandy to warm him from the chill.

"Eliza, I love you. You are my maker. My lover. I know deep down we are not meant to be, for the fates of the Prophecy have spoken. But, I must search out who I am. Where I come from. Will you search with me? I can't do what is asked of me until I find out who I am. So, will you come with me?"

Eliza smiled at him. Her eyes told him that she loved him.

"Yes, I will search with you. We will find your truth together."

The next night, they abandoned the cottage and began the search for his origins. Together.

The End

ABOUT THE AUTHOR

Having been born and raised in Hawaii, I loved telling stories ever since I was a child about vampires, werewolves, angels, demons, and witches. I was a little girl who loved scary stories, much to my mother's dismay. The scarier - the better. Hawaii was a perfect place for stories until I moved to Seattle. I decided to turn a love for the supernatural into writing stories to see if others would love them as much as I do. Currently, I live in Florida but since I'm a Seattle girl at heart, my stories take place in the Northwest. I continue to write supernatural stories of vampires, werewolves, witches, and more while enjoying the beaches and sunshine.